You Have To Write

Also by Janet S. Wong

Grump
Night Garden: Poems from the World of Dreams
Behind the Wheel: Poems About Driving
The Rainbow Hand: Poems About Mothers and Children
A Suitcase of Seaweed and Other Poems
Good Luck Gold and Other Poems

Also Illustrated by Teresa Flavin

Fly High! The Story of Bessie Coleman
The Old Cotton Blues

(Margaret K. McElderry Books)

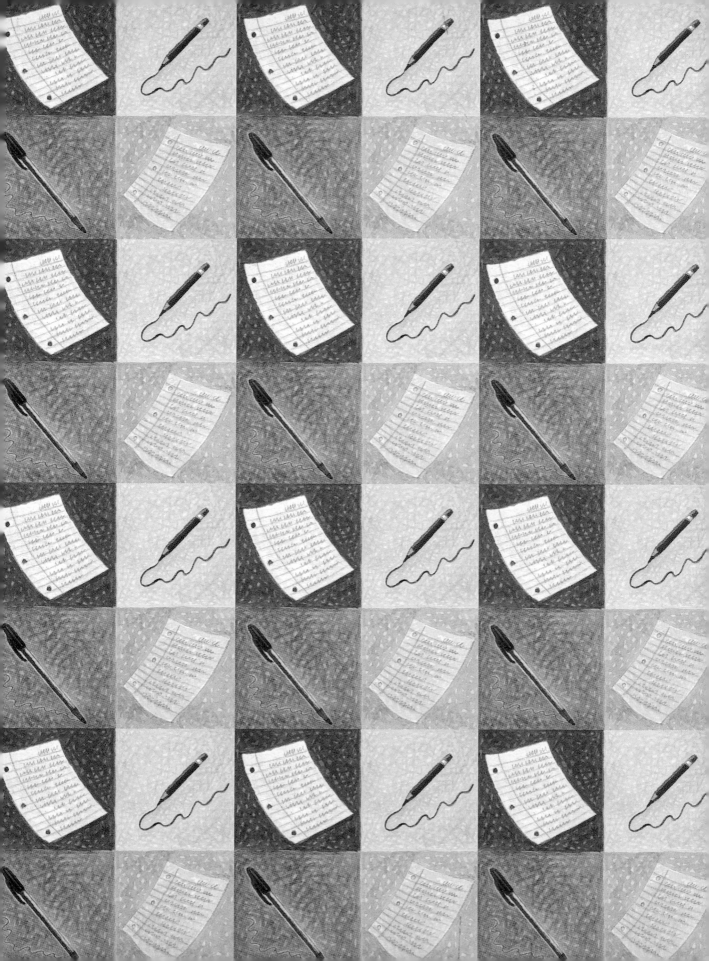

You Have To Write

To The kids
at Sunny Hills,
Write!

by Janet S. Wong
illustrated by Teresa Flavin

Margaret K. McElderry Books
New York London Toronto Sydney Singapore

To Carol Jago
—J. S. W.

For my grandparents
—T. F.

You have to write.
You hate to write.

You want it to be good,
to make us cry
or bust up laughing
when the room is quiet.

You want the laugh
to come from the belly,
a surprise, like a burp
with a smile.

So you look and look and look a while
for something special
to write about,
some magic story.

Your eyes dance around the room,
out the window,
into the hall,
as you look and look and look
all around.

Boy, how the others shine.
She's got a story.
She's been to France.
And him, with his big house, his mother's car—

Wait. Did you forget who you are?

Who else can say what you have seen?
Who else can tell your stories,
and the stories of your mother and your father
and your grandmother and grandfather
and uncles and aunts and cousins,
and your dog and your cat
and the fish you wish you had—

No one else can say
what you have seen
and heard
and felt
today—

but if you tell us well,
very well,
your stories will seem like our own.

Oh, if only you were taller.
If only your family were rich.
If only you lived the good life.

Why do my parents have to fight?

Write about the fights.
Write about the holes in your socks,
your grandmother cracking her knuckles,
your father snoring all night long.

Reach inside.
Write about the dark times.

The rain
soaked the library book
I tried to keep dry
under my coat.
I hid the wet book
in a pile in my room,
almost forgetting the whole mess
until the book started to grow
black spots.
It was a book on flowers,
one spotted lily on the cover,
rotting.

Write about the bright times.

My mother sponged the spots clean
with bleach.
I found some rocks
to press the book
that had paper towels
placed flat inside.

Though it still looked not quite right,
a ripple running through the spine,
our librarian didn't mind
and sent me home
with books on birds,
wrapped in a plastic bag
to keep them from flying away, she said.

Some will call you crazy.
"You think you're so special?"
Go ahead. Be important.
Dream big.

I

Over

Us

Then

Finally

All right, all right, all right, all right, all right,
I'll write.

About

Later
when I think of something—

We

Under

Behind

Write now.
Think now.
Remember.
Take your mind for a walk

back to this morning,
back to yesterday,
back to when you were six,
                    and five,
                         and four,
                              and three,

scared of the wind
in the trees.

I hear a strong wind
and I shiver
between the cold sheets
wondering
if the old tree
outside Mommy's window
will break
and fall
and hurt her, asleep,
and leave me
all alone.

Write about now.
Tonight.
Tomorrow.

Trash today, tomorrow.
It's my job to wheel the can
out to the curb and set it straight,
make sure it's set on level ground.
Can't have it rolling down the hill.

I've got to fill the can just so
to fit the trash we make each week.
If the lid is not on tight,
the crows will pull and tear the bags
and toss the apple cores and bones
everywhere, into the street,
and then the wild dogs will come,
and neighbors walking by will think
I didn't know how to do it right.

Why not think
about the plain,
about the everyday,
the everyday,

even the downright smelly;
this stuff—
the way it really happens?

Make a picture
in your mind,
clear, true.

Move that picture from your mind
down to a piece of paper.

A napkin, or

the back of your hand,

the bottom of your shoe.

Write.

What if
you write the worst string of words ever?
Never fear.
Eat a carrot. Take a nap. Drink water.

Come back
to this piece of work so bad that

there must be a dozen ways
to write it better.
And write it better.
Write it again, on a clean piece of paper.
Twist your ideas. Stretch.
Snatch new words out of nowhere.

Make your words move.
Make your words dance,

five or ten or fifteen times,
fifty different dances,
if you're strong.

And lay each piece of paper out
on a long stretch of floor
and pluck the best parts
out of each piece,

Weave
them together—
half of Draft 1, a word from Draft 4,
a whole line from number 5.

Try.

Because you have to write,
and you want it to be good.

Margaret K. McElderry Books

An imprint of Simon & Schuster Children's Publishing Division

1230 Avenue of the Americas, New York, New York 10020

Text copyright © 1998, 2002 by Janet S. Wong

Illustrations copyright © 2002 by Teresa Flavin

Portions of the text of this book originally appeared in *Instructor* magazine (Scholastic) as part
of the "Young Writer's Workshop" series by Joan Novelli (August 1997- May/June 1998).

All rights reserved, including the right of reproduction in whole or in part in any form.

Book design by Abelardo Martínez

The text for this book is set in Cantoria.

The illustrations are rendered in gouache on paper.

Manufactured in China

6 8 10 9 7 5

Library of Congress Cataloging-in-Publication Data

Wong, Janet S.

You have to write / by Janet S. Wong ; illustrated by Teresa Flavin.

p. cm.

ISBN 0-689-83409-8

1. Creative writing—Juvenile poetry. 2. Children's poetry, American. [1. Creative writing—
Poetry. 2. Authorship—Poetry. 3. American poetry.] I. Flavin, Teresa, ill. II. Title.

PS3573.O578 Y68 2002

811'.54—dc21

2001030810

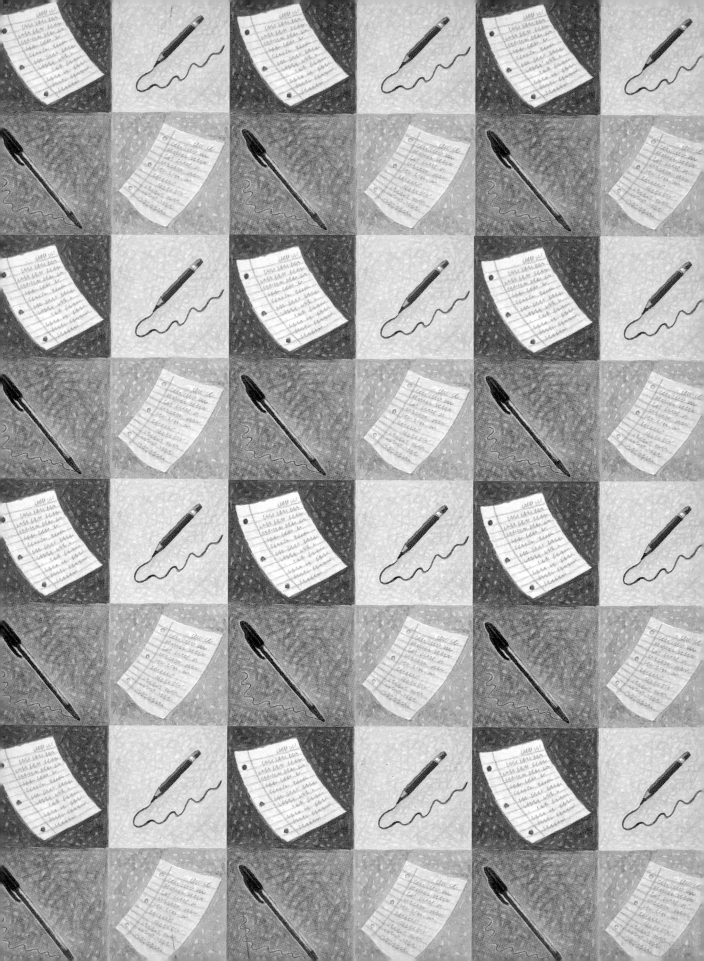